Rose's Heart's Decision

Phyllis A. Collmann

Library of Congress Control Number: 2005902901

ISBN: 1-57579-308-3

Printed in the United States of America
Pine Hill Press
4000 West 57th Street
Sioux Falls, SD 57106

‿⁊ *Dedication* ⁊‿

To my husband Colin, for 53 years of marriage
And for his devoted love and support.
To my children
Cynthia, Kimberly, Ronald and Melonie
I love each one of you best.

A Very Special Thank You

Julie Ann Madden
Diane Ten Napel
Nicole Collmann

Cover
Karen Taylor Mortensen

Thank you Larry and Darlene Tentinger
Thank you to the Le Mars City Council

About the Author

Phyllis A. Collmann is a retired nurse. She lives on a farm with her husband of 53 years. This is the third about Rose Donlin. It is a sequel to her first and second pioneer book. The first book is called *Rose's Betrayal and Survival*. The second book is called *Rose's Triumpant Return*. And the third book is called *Rose's Heart's Decision*.

Published Books:

Rose's Betrayal and Survival
Rose's Triumphant Return
Rose's Heart's Decision
Kim's Unplanned Saga
Mother's Innocence Proven

Rose's Heart's Decision

PHYLLIS A. COLLMANN takes you on another exciting adventure. The year is 1885. A new man enters her life. But the memory of Henry Helgens is strong in her heart. Join rose as she struggles to help a black man. Her on going struggles to build the Higgens hospital and library.

"You must read about Rose Donlin's thrilling adventures."

—*Nicole Collmann*

"Very interesting and very entertaining."

—*Diane Ten Napel*

"A pioneer story filled with love, adventure and also sorrow."

—*Kim Bonnett*

"As the saga continues love deepens but will Rose chose love or her protector? Readers will delight in discovering Collmann's answer."

—*Julie Ann Madden*

⁓ Chapter 1 ⁓

Rose's heart felt heavy. And she was not sleeping at night. When she did fall asleep she would have a restless dream. The dream was always the same. She was always riding on the beautiful horse she had taken from the man that had kidnapped her from the train. Henry Helgens was always riding beside her. She could reach out and touch him. It was when she reached out for him, Rose would awaken and then the long night would begin. The memories of the months she had spent with Henry were so fresh in her mind. Each detail was remembered and treasured. One memory took one minute but that minute out of the month of traveling was the best, and the memory would keep Rose awake until early in the morning.

Each morning Rose slipped out of the boarding house wearing her hat with the black lace hiding her face. Rose walked swiftly to the telegraph office not wanting to be seen by anyone. She always asked the young man, who was so willing to help her, if she had received news from the sheriff.

The telegram Rose had sent was to help her locate the Henry Helgens family. She owed Henry's family her life letting her escape from being kidnapped the second time by a cruel man who wanted her for his own. The young man in the telegraph office greeted her warmly but the news was again the same. He had not heard from the sheriff. Rose thanked him, then quietly left.

The walk back to her room with the same news each day was always a let down for her. The large amount of money was lying on her nightstand still wrapped in a towel. The money was to be given to the Helgens' family for using all of their savings to get her away from the man and for saving her life.

Chapter 2

The sun was shining brightly through the boarding house window. She felt a need to get out for fresh air, to stop the feeling of being trapped. Rose yearned to see the cabin one more time. Her feelings were pulling her toward the stable.

The stable hand was taking good care of the precious horse. He harnessed the horse and helped Rose up into the buggy. She continually urged the horse to go faster toward the edge of town. It was all so familiar. As soon as she was out in the open countryside Rose took off her large black velvet hat and long black veil. Her hair was growing out again in the two months since she had cut it completely off. It felt good to let the wind blow against her face and hair.

Chapter 3

Rose pulled back on the reins as she approached Joseph's land. Stopping the horse just as the back of the buggy was standing on the beginning of the land that was now hers.

This was where it had all started. It felt different now. At first, five and one-half years ago, John Fitzspatrick had told her they were on Joseph Higgins' land. At that time nothing made any sense to her. Rose was seventeen years old. Everything was so strange to her. She had felt that was the end of her life.

Without her knowing, an old chapter had closed. A new chapter was opening up to her. Rose Donlin's new life would bring her things she had only read and dreamed of. The feeling of being free came over her and she began to cry. Her life had changed again and she knew she had to make a new plan for her life.

Rose was busy thinking and then she realized how close she was to the cabin. She pulled back on the reins and the giant horse slowed to a slow walk. She approached the last knoll and she could see the roof of the cabin, barn and corral.

Rose stopped the horse for a minute to take in the memory that was so vivid in her mind.

The sight brought out emotions she wanted to forget and not feel. Five and one-half years is a long time in a young girl's life. Joseph Higgins had not made it easy for her. He had expected her to work like a man. When Rose had accomplished his demands, Joseph began to change his harshness to acknowledging Rose Donlin was a very special person. Joseph knew it within a few months after Rose arrived at his cabin.

 Chapter 4

She stepped down out of the buggy, tied her horse to the hitching post and stepped upon the same steps she had repaired after the first day, five and one-half years ago. Rose's hand went out and touched the rusty iron door knob. The door's wood was dry and filled with cracks. Little pieces of the wood curled up from old age.

Joseph's father had started building the cabin after he had staked out his 3000 acres of land. Joseph's mother had waited in a room back of a butcher shop in Oklahoma City, working as a cook in a restaurant of the boarding house, while her husband rode his horse around his new land. He pounded in tree limbs to mark his homestead land. He also drew a map and when he returned to Oklahoma City, he registered his 3000 acres of land. The year was 1818.

Rose paused and then slowly opened the door. Her body jerked when the rusty hinges made a squeak as she opened the door only enough to squeeze in. The inside was completely dark as she had asked the nearest renter to board up the windows. Rose had wanted no one to be able to look in or be able to break in. She had also asked the renter to check the homestead every couple of days. Stepping into the cabin she noted nothing had changed. It looked the same as the day she had shut the door and left for St. Louis. Rose lit the lamp and stood in the middle of the room and took time to look. Joseph's bed stood along the fireplace. Next to it was the old wooden rocking chair his father had made for his mother when she discovered a baby was on the way. The baby had been Joseph, born in 1820.

Chapter 5

Nothing had been easy for Joseph's parents. Joseph told Rose stories of how they had survived. Eating had to be planned for the entire year. But mostly for the long winter months. Joseph's mother raised as much of their food as she could. It was picked from the garden then stored raw in the cave. Joseph told Rose a story about his father helping with the setting hens. He had built small enclosed boxes from scraps of lumber. When he found hens setting and beginning to lay their eggs he would carry the hen and her eggs into one of his boxes and lock her in. This went on until he had all of his boxes filled with setting hens. Once a day each hen was allowed out to eat and drink. Joseph told Rose how fascinated his father was over each hen knowing exactly what box it came out of. Then when the hen was done eating and drinking, she again would return to her box. He said the hen would walk over her eggs, fluff out her feathers and gently spread herself over her many eggs. Joseph said he remembered even when being a small boy how excited his father would get when the chicks began to hatch. Saving the chicks meant eggs when they grew to hens and also meat when food was low. By spring the food in the cave would be running out and a hen would be their food.

Chapter 6

Joseph's father had only one horse when he homesteaded his land. He rode bareback into Oklahoma City to buy his supplies. The supplies were tied over the back of his horse and then he would walk home leading the horse.

Joseph told Rose his mother rarely left the homestead. With only the one horse he said she was always busy at home. She cooked over the fireplace and then sewed by hand the rest of the day. The feed sacks were made into her dresses and Joseph and his father got a new shirt when the sacks were empty. She would go to the creek and wash the feed sacks before starting to cut out the shirts. His mother had no pattern except the dress and shirts they wore.

Rose looked at the large square table in the middle of the cabin. She remembered Joseph telling her how his father had worked for days cutting large tree limbs down, then asking one of his renters to haul the huge tree limbs into Oklahoma City to the lumber mill. He had eight boards made for the top of the table. When the boards were brought back to the cabin, a frame was made and the top boards were fastened to it. Joseph explained how his father cut smaller limbs and crafted designs into them and made the table legs. Times were hard for them.

Rose wished Joseph's parents could have enjoyed the wealth that she had now. She would never let the Higgins name be forgotten in all of Oklahoma. Joseph had told Rose the lamp was purchased long after the cabin was completed. The first year they had no light in the cabin at night. The only light would come from the wood burning in the fireplace.

When Joseph's father received rent money, one item had been brought home to the cabin at a time.

๛ Chapter 7 ๛

Men traveling, either walking or on horseback who stopped and asked for a meal would work a day or would stay for a small penace. Joseph's father then had help to build fences and dig the cave. Joseph reminisced to Rose about the day all of the renters came to build the barn and corral. Looking back, Joseph admitted the best time of his life had been watching the barn being built. The men always had such a good time working together. The days were hot and the summer weather dry. The food was cooked over the fireplace. The door of the cabin was always open and the windows removed from the cabin. The food had to be planned ahead so no man went hungry. Each woman brought food and helped to serve the men. The children of each family came. This was, as Joseph told her, a way for the young children getting to play with their neighbors. Large families with older sons sent their boys to school until they were old enough to work at home in the field. Some boys stopped going to school when they reached the age of eight years old. The young boys worked along side of their fathers and learned how to build the barns. By noon the young energetic boys could eat as much as their fathers. Rose listened to all of Joseph's stories knowing it brought joy to him to talk about his life. Rose walked over to the rocking chair and sat down remembering how she felt when Joseph said,"The best time of my life now is having you here with me." She also realized at that time her liking of him had been growing too. Joseph had lived most of his life, and hers was just beginning.

Chapter 8

Nothing could have surprised her more when the barking of a dog sounded close to the cabin. Then Rose heard a wagon and horse's hooves coming near the porch.

When Rose slowly opened the cabin door Pal was jumping and barking. She got down on her knees and let him lick her face as she knew he was as happy to see her as she was to see him. The renter had come to check the cabin. Now Rose had her companion back. Joseph had brought him home for her from one of his trips to town. She would never leave him again. Pal would travel with her from this time on.

Rose explained to her renter she would keep Pal with her. Pal sensed he was not leaving, he walked to the rocking chair and laid down. She immediately began talking to him. Rose felt he remembered he was home.

Rose sat down in the chair beside him. She began by telling Pal how much she missed Joseph being in the cabin with them. Pal rose to his feet and walked to Joseph's bed and put his head on the bed next to the pillow. She sat quietly and watched as Pal checked the cabin out. He sniffed and smelled over the entire cabin. Rose had no doubt Pal knew and remembered where he was.

As Rose stood up, Pal was at the door. Without her realizing, an old fear was not first in her thoughts. She was thinking of walking over the homestead. Rose was not alone now.

Rose found the barn and corral had not changed. The only change was more birds and small animals had moved in. The birds were wildly chirping, making sure each one was heard. She thought they all sounded content.

The path to the creek was clear and easy to see. Rose had used the path many times a day. Carrying water or leading the horses to the creek over the path had been a daily chore. Pal was running ahead but only a few feet at a time. Then he would stop and wait for her to catch up.

⟨ Chapter 9 ⟩

Rose stood at the edge of the creek. It was not the feeling she had expected. She gazed out over the water. The feeling of home sickness came over her. Tiny little tears ran down her cheeks. Pal looked up at her face and sensed her sadness. He sat down at the bottom of her skirt next to her feet. Rose walked along the edge of the creek that brought back so many memories. She knew the exact location where she had delivered the Indian baby. Rose felt coming back here was what she had to do to be able to move on in her life. She decided no one would come here, or take anything, until she was ready to deal with it. Rose walked back toward the cabin. The cave door was closed as she had left it. Lifting the door had never been easy for her. It had been made with heavy thick boards to keep animals from sneaking in. Also, Joseph had told her the strong winds and winter storms would not be able to pull it open and spoil the precious, needed food.

As she proceeded toward the cabin, her eyes looked over at the tiny cross sticking up out of the small space that had been cleared for the grave of Joseph's baby sister.

Joseph had been so reluctant to even talk about it. Rose remembered she had been there nearly two years before he would talk about any of his early memories of the death of his precious baby sister.

He was nearly seven years old when his mother told him about the baby coming the following spring. He told Rose how happy his parents were. His mother sewed all of the baby's clothes by hand. She was prepared by spring.

Joseph said his parents talked alot that winter about the baby coming. The name had been chosen.

After she had found the small cross she had tried many times through the two years to read the name. The name had been carved in the cross but over the years the name had almost disappeared. The small letters read. Martha Gertrude Higgins, Born 1827 Died 1827.

Rose was so curious about why the day date had not been added to the cross. Joseph surprised her by his answer. They did not know what day it had been.

Joseph told Rose he had awakened to hear his parents talking and their voices sounded anxious and louder than normal. He slipped out of bed and quietly opened his bedroom door. He could see his father trying to comfort his mother. What Joseph did not know was his mother had labored all night. Joseph had never witnessed his father so frightened as he appeared to be.

His father instructed him to get to the nearest renter's wife. Joseph ran four miles as fast as he could. Years later, he was still blaming himself for not getting help sooner.

When he returned to the cabin with the renter's wife, he found his mother and father crying uncontrollably. The baby girl they had looked forward to for nine months, had died. Martha Gertrude Higgins did not survive the long labored birth.

Joseph mentioned how the mourning of the baby by his parents appeared to a seven year old, they were both in pain. He said he tried to be quiet and he spent more time outside doing the chores for his father.

Joseph was allowed nearly two weeks off from his home schooling until his mother recuperated.

Joseph had said many times how hard a life his mother had had. She had no woman to talk to. She had left her parents to travel with her new young husband many miles away from them. He also told Rose he had only seen his grandparents once before they had died of Diphtheria.

Sitting beside the cross next to a clump of the tiny blue violets, Rose remembered asking Joseph for the flower seeds on one of his trips into Oklahoma City after he told her about the baby. All the sad memories were emerging from her mind.

Chapter 10

Pal stood up, stretched and began moving over her lap. Rose looked up and knew she needed to return to the boarding house as the sun would be down by the time she arrived back to her room.

Her horse had drunk from the creek and eaten grass. Rose hitched her horse up to the buggy and started back toward Oklahoma City with Pal running along side.

Rose was nearly back to the road that led off her land, when Pal jolted forward and ran off the road, barking and running in a frenzy. The first sight Rose had was of a bloody body lying crumpled up, with Pal running relentlessly around the body, growling.

Leaping out of the buggy, Rose ran to the body. The sight was almost unbearable. The body had blood seaping out of every opening on his head. His face was swollen and a large bump was protruding out on his forehead. He could open one eye about halfway. The other eye was puffed closed with blood running down out of it.

He had no shirt or shoes on. He wore only a pair of pants that were torn up past his knees. He looked as if someone had whipped him and left him here to die. Whoever had done this felt sure no one would stop and care for a Black man.

He was moaning and groaning in severe agonizing pain. The violent anger of a person or persons had committed this crime. He looked up to see a beautiful white girl looking back at him. Rose was almost repulsed by what she saw. The only thing she could say was, "I'm going to help you, sir."

Rose pulled her giant horse next to the wounded man. She told the man he had to help to get up in the buggy. After several tries, the man slumped into the buggy.

Rose turned the horse around and headed back to the homestead. She urged the horse close to the edge of the creek. The man tried to get out of the buggy, finally falling to the ground. She told him he had to get into the water to wash all of the open wounds. The splash into the water and then the man disappeared under the water. Rose approached the edge and was ready to jump in when he came to the surface. He grunted in agony while slowly struggling onto the shore and lying face down. She dropped to her knees and tried to gently, but firmly, roll him over so he would not suffocate. Rose's determination to help this nearly dead man was what encouraged the man to help her. He pulled himself half-way into the buggy. She returned to the cabin and he tried to slip back out of the buggy. He crumpled to the ground, screaming in pain. She yelled at him to crawl into the cabin. Opening the door for him and telling him he had to do this and when she finally had him in Joseph's bed, Rose covered the broken, beaten man. Then quickly ran to the barn for Joseph's horse salve. Trying not to give him more pain, Rose applied salve to every open protruding cut. The sounds he made were low, miserable, quivering noises. She gently covered him and said, "Do not try and get up. I'll be back early in the morning. You must not be seen. Do not open the door. Do not make any noise. I promise I'll be back."

⌒✑ Chapter 11 ✑⌒

Pal was waiting outside of the cabin door for her. She snapped her fingers and he hopped up into the buggy beside her because the trip would be fast. The stable hand was waiting for her. He unharnessed the big horse and led him to the back of the stable, an area where no one else was allowed.

Rose had her large black hat on with the lace down over her face. She hurried along to the back of the boarding house. Quietly, entering the door with Pal. She took two steps at a time to the second floor. Then stopped at her father's door. Rose tapped on the door and opened it slowly. Saying, "Father, it's Rose." Louis Donlin was recouperating from his eye surgery. He greeted Rose, telling her how he thought he could see small objects now. For a minute, the good news took her mind off of the man lying in Joseph's bed in the cabin.

Louis Donlin laughed and said, "Rose, why do I think I'm seeing a dog?" "Because, Father, you are." Rose was so happy, that her father was able to see again.

After saying "good-night," Rose and Pal slipped next door to her room. Pal waited for Rose to go to sleep and he laid on a rug next to her bed. Rose's mind would not rest until she had figured out just how she could help a Black man who lie near death from a beating that had been meant to kill him.

Pal woke Rose early. He needed to go outside. She dressed putting on her hat and veil. Once outside Pal walked next to her as she headed to the telegraph office. The young man knew what Rose had came for. He handed her a paper.

Surprising her, she hesitated while reaching out to take the paper from him. Rose folded the paper and slipped it into her draw string bag. She thanked the young man.

He said, "Miss, are you going to read it? In case you need to return a message."

"Sir, I'm going to my room to read it. If I need to send another message, I'll return," Rose answered softly. No matter what the message said, Rose thought she would need time to think about an answer.

Rose walked as fast as she could to the boarding house, and with no one in sight she lifted her skirt and ran up the steps to the second floor. She hurriedly went into her room and sat on the edge of her bed. Rose began opening the crumbled telegram that she had squeezed together in her bag. Rose stared at each word. Then went back several times and reread the message. The sheriff knew the Helgens family and also knew their location. Rose reached out and petted Pal's head, and said, "We know where he is now." The answer to the telegram would have to wait.

Chapter 12

The defenseless lonely unknown man in her cabin needed her help first. Rose took her father to the boarding house dining room and she ordered a large breakfast but ate a very small portion. The left over food and biscuits were put into her napkin and carefully slid into her bag. Her father's eye sight was improving and he had been able to watch Rose take the food from the table but had no idea why.

She escorted her father safely back to his room and told him she would return to take him to lunch.

The clouds threatening rain over head made her hurry along the street to the stable. It took only a few minutes for the livery stable hand to bring the big horse from the back and hitch him to the buggy. The horse seemed to sense a storm was on the way. He wanted to run, but Rose did not want to be noticed. She held him back until she was a short distance from town. Then she let him run like he wanted. The first stop Rose made after getting to her land was to a renter and she asked to buy some eggs. A couple hens. The hen's legs were tied together for the ride to the cabin. Pal reached the cabin first, barking as if he knew he was home. Before Rose tied the big horse to the hiching post she noticed the door was ajar a few inches and Pal pushed with his nose and was inside. Pal's bark sounded urgent, and angry. Rose stepped in and the bed was empty. Pal ran to her and then back to a corner in the cabin. In the darkness Rose could make out a figure hiding in the corner.

She lit the lamp and the man was on his knees with his face to the floor. Some of his open areas were still bleeding. He slowly lifted his head and appeared to see her with blurred vision. He began to mumble and Rose heard him say, "Praise God, hers back." Rose spoke softly, saying, "I'm so sorry you're afraid. Please let me help you. I brought you food." She sat down on the floor next to him. Rose could see the open areas were draining and she knew she had to get this man back to the creek to cleanse him again. She was sure he needed to eat before she could move him.

Feeding him was a slow process. His neck looked as if someone had put a rope around this man's throat and dragged him. His throat was red and raw with skin torn open. Rose gave him small pieces of food to swallow. With each swallow his face grimaced with discomfort. He was so hungry he would swallow and immediately open his mouth for the next bite. When the last bite of food was gone. Rose waited and then said, "Sir, we need to go to the creek and wash your open areas with lye soap. So I can fill all of your wounds with fresh salve again." He opened the eye he could open and stared at her in a way that showed her how doubtful he felt he could do this.

Chapter 13

Rose told the Black man to crawl to the door and out onto the porch. She unhitched the horse from the buggy. The horse was placed so crawling over from the porch and onto the horse's back was possible. He could lay on the blanket Rose placed for him.

Because this was so painful, and the sores were opening up from crawling on the wooden floor and porch, blood was running down his legs. Rose could hear thunder off in the distance, so she knew she had to hurry. Rose knew the creek very well. She walked the horse into very shallow water along the bank and lowered the man that needed help so badly. He laid on the bottom submerged in water with only his face showing. She sat in the water next to him fully clothed to make sure he didn't drown. The water was warm on the top from the sun but cool on the bottom. Rose could see on his face how he had relaxed and the soothing cool water made her think his excruciating pain had eased up. She placed the rag and lye soap in his hand and he slowly moved his hand to wash his wounds.

After he had finished, Rose struggled to get the man out of the water and upon the grassy bank. Then she struggled to get the man upon the back of her large horse. The man moaned all the way to the cabin. Rose was again determined to get the man back into Joseph's bed. Then she needed to apply salve on all of his painful openings. She pleaded with him to stay in bed. He tried to explain why the door of the cabin was unlocked and why he was on the floor sitting in the corner. In a voice sounding gravely and almost inaudable.

He said, "Me heared a sound, aun me thunk, them ornery folk was come to kil me. Me crawl to th door and spied ou. Me seed a dark skinned maan."

Rose was stunned. Her breath caught in her throat. She did not say a word. She covered the man and then told him she would return the next day with food. She also reminded him not to open the door. If he needed to go out, he must go out through the smoke house.

Rose quickly walked to the door and reached for the handle. Then turned back and in a strained voice asked if he had seen only one dark skinned man outside of the cabin. The answer, was in a whisper that she could not hear, but he moved his head slightly. Indicating yes.

⤳ Chapter 14 ⤵

The big horse did not have to be encouraged. It was one of the fastest rides in a buggy she had ever had. Rose pulled her hat and veil down hard on her head and over her face.

Her father was waiting. She tried to clear her mind of what she knew was true. The kidnapper was back and he knew where she was.

Louis Donlin informed Rose he was ready to go home to St. Louis. She tried to talk him into staying another week, but he had made up his mind.

Now, she needed to convince her father to get off of the train in a town that Rose had recieved the telegram from. She asked her father to deliever a package to the sheriff. Louis Donlin sat listening and looking directly into his daughter's eyes. He could hear in her voice how serious she was. He owed her so much he would never think of refusing her.

Rose packed the money securely in a box so it would be easy for her father to carry. Inside she placed a letter to the family that had given their life savings to save her from the kidnapper. One part was addressed to Henry. She poured her heart out to him about how much she had missed him when he had left. She mentioned how he had protected her on their month-long trip together. She wanted to also mention the kiss they had shared but the letter would be read by all of his family, so she left out that part.

Rose waited with her father in her room until she knew she could get him aboard the train, say good-bye and hurry back to her room because her face would not be covered with her hat and black veil. Rose hugged and kissed her father and reassured him she would be home to see him soon.

⤚ Chapter 15 ⤙

The food she ordered at the boarding house was a large amount. She asked that it be put into the tin pie plates she had purchased from the general store. The pie tins were covered with white dish towels and carried to the buggy in a large bag. Her giant steed always needed to run after his long night of being locked up. When the edge of town appeared Rose loosened the reins and his excitement showed. He would throw his head up and nothing could stop him. Pal ran in front until the big hooves sounded close and then he would run along the side. Rose did not try to slow her horse back. She just held on. Her mind was thinking about and missing her father. After putting her horse and buggy out of sight in the corral she opened the cabin door. Even in the darkness inside the cabin, Rose could see a figure lying in Joseph's bed. She stood still waiting for her eyes to adjust to the darkness. The man raised his bruised and battered head up and knew it was Rose, and laid his head back on his pillow in relief. The globe on the lamp was covered with black smoke letting out a small amount of light after Rose lit it. She had not had time to clean it. The only white she could see was the Black man's eyes. She prepared the Black man to eat the food she had brought for him.

The painful sores had healing scabs on them. He was able to sit up at the table. Rose had been aware he was a large man but she had not seen him stand up straight. He had always been bent over or crawling on the floor or ground.

When Rose stood the man up she was afraid his head would touch the top of the cabin ceiling. She looked down at his bare feet and she wondered if anyone made shoes to fit feet that large.

The plate of food was in front of him. Rose put the spoon in his hand. He could not hold the spoon with his fingers. He dropped the spoon on the table and used his fingers. Rose could tell that was how he had always eaten. His large hands showed broken fingers that had healed with knots on them. Gnarls on each hand as if someone had hit them with a hammer.

When he had his plate nearly clean, he stopped and licked his fingers. Then lifted his head and looked directly at Rose.

She spoke first and asked, "What is your name? What do people call you?"

Rose thought he said, "Giant."

"That is not your given name," she continued.

He sat in silence, then as if remembering said, "Me mammy yipped, Rufus George."

"Rufus be me pappies call. Me pappie be a black slave. "George, be a prsdent." His words were slurred and some words were not understandable.

"Then I will call you Rufus George." Rose said.

He was so nervous and tried to make Rose understand. "Me go, Me go." He raised his hand and pointed a broken finger at her, and said, "Mam, you get sore, you get sore. Go now, Go now." Rufus George stumbled through the words.

"No, no," Rose said, in a firm and determined voice. "You are going to be my guard. You will drive my buggy." The cabin was so quiet, only breathing of air could be heard. Even Pal turned his head.

Rufus George put his head down. He didn't want to disobey her but he thought she had no idea how cruel people would be to her. His skin was very black and her skin was as fair as an angel. This was unheard of in 1885.

Rose had made up her mind. But what Rose did not know was what a big mistake she was making. She had known unhappiness, loneliness, rejection. Now she was about to learn what hate was, what violence was. One man against another.

Rose instructed Rufus George to stay in the cabin until she returned the next day. She had a plan and she needed to get help from all of her many renters. Most of the day she traveled from one homestead to the next.

Rose felt they had accepted her explanation of why the big Black man was living in her cabin. Some showed her their anger and hate but she also knew they did not want to lose their homestead, so they would do what was expected of them. Rose asked each family to come to her cabin. The entire family was to come the following morning to meet Rufus George. Rose's night was long and seemingly endless. She arrived at the cabin with food she had promised him. Rufus George ate his breakfast like a man who had not eaten in many days. She would need to bring more food. The clothes Rose brought from the general store was the largest size in the store. She could not let anyone see him with bare skin showing.

She looked at him and she saw more white in his eyes than before. He also acted very nervous.

When he heard the first wagon arrive his eyes looked larger than ever. He went immediately to sit on the floor in a dark corner of the cabin. The horses and wagons could be heard coming from a mile away. The knock on the door was unexpected as all the renters and their families stayed in their wagons. Rose looked over at Rufus George and motioned for him to sit on a chair. She slowly opened the door to find John Fitzpatrick standing there looking very troubled. John stepped in and could not take his eyes off of her. Then he saw something move out of the corner of his eyes. He jerked around and saw Rufus George as Rufus stood up.

Nothing prepared him for seeing this large Black man in Rose's cabin. Rose yelled, "John, this is Rufus George, he is working for me."

John Fitzpatrick opened his mouth and she had never seen this type of reaction from him. She remained motionless keeping her eyes fixed on John as Rufus George came closer. John's face was twisted in a frown. Rufus George put his head down but at the same time stretched his hand out to John.

Rose knew what was happening at this very moment and to avoid hurting Rufus George she stepped up to Rufus George and took his hand. She stood with her lilly white hand in this huge very Black hand. John had just refused to shake hands with Rufus George. The clatter of wagons and horses whinnying broke the awkward silence.

Rose, gripped Rufus George's hand hard as he was pulling his hand away. She pulled him to the door. Rose needed every man, women and child to see Rufus George was a friend that was going to help her build the hospital and later the library. John was left standing alone in the cabin. Rose walked to each wagon with Rufus George. Each person met the man that was the very opposite of what they were. She explained Rufus George would live in her cabin with Pal and all of Joseph's guns. He would be treated with kindness and no one would be allowed to shun him.

Chapter 16

Rose could see some of the women lean toward their husbands. Mothers were holding their children close. The biggest surprise to each family as Rose pulled this giant Black man to them,where the tears running down his face. He was so frightened and afraid they would turn against Rose. But that was not going to happen, for Rose had been most generous to each family.

One small girl standing along side of her father's wagon darted toward Rufus George. He extended his hand and she laid her hand in his. Pulling her hand back, she quickly looked down at it. She had never seen a Black man. Rose was certain the girl had expected to see black on her hand.

Walking to the next wagon, a young man jumped out away from his family. The man ran to Rufus George as every settler watched closely.

Rose's Heart's Decision

The man named Toby said, "Rufus George, I want to help you build Rose Donlin's hospital and library."

After each wagon rumbled out of the farm yard, Rose and Rufus George returned to the cabin to find John Fitzpatrick was gone. Rose felt a small amount of sadness.

Rose explained to Rufus George again not to leave the cabin. Her thoughts were to keep him safe. When Rose left the cabin with her horse eager to run, she headed toward the homestead of the young man. She hoped he would come and live in Joseph's cabin and protect Rufus George, as well as working with him. The meeting went well. Rose felt confident the two men could become friends. On the rest of the trip home she wished it was Henry Helgens with Rufus George.

The food she purchased would fill a buckboard. The young man opened the cabin door and Rufus George stepped out to carry the 50 pound bags in. He could carry twice as much weight at one time as an average man.

Chapter 17

Rose needed to study and stake out the ground on which the hospital would be built. It would be located on the edge of her land and also on the edge of Oklahoma City. While Rose was at the lumber yard, Rufus George and Toby began the job of digging the foundation with shovels, axes and hoes.

Before noon, most of the men who rented Rose's land came to help. Every few feet a man chopped the soil with a pickaxe to loosen the soil. The next man scooped the loose dirt out and away.

When the mule arrived, Rufus George asked if he could drive the mule that was hitched to a steel plow. The plow would make a deeper furrow to pour a foundation. Rufus George told the owner of the mule he had started driving his pappy's mule when his pappy worked as a slave on a plantation.

The foundation material was brought out by a young dark skinned man with black hair.

Rufus George looked closely at him and then remembered where he had seen him before. This man was the one that had been to Joseph's cabin. Rufus George stopped the mule and grunted at Toby.

Toby was more than eager to drive the mule instead of breaking up the ground with his axe.

Rufus George's steps toward Rose were like his giant size. His life had been full of fear. His father had been a slave on a huge plantation. His mother was also a slave owned by the same man. The owner of the plantation believed in slavery at that time. So all of Rufus George's family worked as slaves. They all lived in a small one room shanty. Every shanty was overcrowded. The children slept on the floor on rugs made with scraps of material from the plantation owners' family's new clothing. When Rufus George reached Rose, he stood like a pillar in front of her. His body blocked out any vision of her. Pal had been running around getting attention from all of the men. He ran up to Rose behind Rufus George with his tail wagging and looking up at her. In a stern voice Rose whispered to him, "Stay, Pal, stay." He stopped dead still and dropped to the ground. He lay in a protective position, ready to pounce.

The dark-skinned man stood looking in every direction, searching for Rose Donlin. His eyes looked at each man. He was looking for and wanting the young woman he had taken from the train. The woman that had tricked him, outsmarted him and had taken his prized possession. The only thing he ever truly loved, his horse.

This was not the first time Rufus George had tried to protect a woman. He was five years old when he noticed the men at the plantation looking and watching his mammy as she worked in the mansion. He saw white men reach out and touch her as they walked by her. To Rufus George this was not right. She belonged to his pappy. After that he spent time checking on his mammy. He would sneak into the kitchen through the back door. This went on in his life until he began to grow so fast and no longer could he not be seen. And he was told to work in the fields with the other slaves. The dark-skinned man missed his horse and wanted him back. He also wanted the young blond haired woman back. He dreamed of riding into his camp in Mexico with her on the back of his magnificent horse. He imagined how the bandits would envy him. She was not only beautiful but strong to work in the camp. She could also bear him many sons.

Without a warning, a gust of wind blew across the ground toward Rose, and before she could grab her skirt, it blew out from behind Rufus George. Rose reached for her skirt to tuck it down between her legs. The dark-skinned man stared at Rufus George hoping to see what he imagined was the blond haired woman he wanted so badly. He stood staring but saw nothing more. Then someone yelled at him to move his wagon. He left toward the direction of Oklahoma City to return to the lumber yard.

Rose Donlin remained hidden behind Rufus George until the dark-skinned man was completely out of sight. Rufus George moved, Rose took two fast steps to his one step, staying hidden until he reached the buggy. Then he turned and picked her up and set her in her buggy. Every man's eye was staring in disbelief. Rufus George spoke, he spoke softly to Rose saying, "mame, ya gtta dig in sumewhare. Me cen, Me cen putt thas booaard op far ya, mame." Rose Donlin knew what Rufus George said was true. He could build the hospital and library with Toby's help. She would have to find a place to hide. The dark-skinned man's insistant behavior demonstrated his unwillingness to give her up.

Chapter 18

While Rufus George talked to Rose in the buggy, Toby was telling all of the renters about the relentless man after Rose. One of the men told Toby to take Rose to old Mrs. Carlisen. No one would ever find her there he said, and if they did they would never leave there. Toby agreed. Old Mrs. Carlisen's place would be the best and only place for Rose to hide. The dark-skinned man would never leave there alive.

Toby knew the stories about old Mrs. Carlisen were not all true but he also knew first hand some were. Toby was the only one who really knew her. Joseph had tried to help her when the accident happened. She even kicked him off of the land she and her beloved rented from him. Toby was only four years old when he wandered away from home and found something that would change his short life.

Toby had gone to her cabin and then stayed with her until she laid her husband to rest. He was the only one she would let near her. Toby took her hand in his small hand and stood by her while they lowered the only man she had ever loved.

Old Mrs. Carlisen watched Toby grow into a handsome young man. He came to her cabin each day after his chores were done at home. Then he would help her lay the seeds of her crop in the rows she had made by hand.

He had helped old Mrs. Carlisen farm her land since the terrible accident. She had lived alone and farmed the land and Toby was the only person she had seen in years. The only person she would let on her land. She had chosen to close herself off from the rest of the world.

Toby stopped the buggy on the dirt lane. He told Rose he would walk the rest of the way into the homestead and tell old Mrs Carlisen about Rose Donlin.

It was dark out and Toby could see only the lamp light through her window. He got to the door and called out her name. He also yelled out his name. The door slowly open and Toby could see the barrel of her shotgun sticking out. Pointing right at his heart and he had seen her shoot before. He had watched her shoot rabbits on the run so he knew she would never miss.

Chapter 19

"Toby, is that you?"

"Yes, yes, it sure as hell is," was Toby's quick nervous reply. "What are you doing here at this time of night? Are you in some kind of trouble?" She asked in a loud voice.

"No, I brought someone for you to meet. I thought maybe you'd let her stay with you for a time." Toby said in a pleading voice. Rose was standing behind Toby, trying to keep Pal quiet.

It was silent for what Toby thought would be a no. Then he heard her say, "Alright, but just for a time. Is this your woman?" Toby did not answer.

The two women stood a few feet away from each other just staring.

Rose looked into the eyes of a small thin lonely old woman. Her life showed on her face and body. She could no longer stand up straight. Her shoulders bent forward from hard work over the years. Her hands were chapped and her fingernails were broken off and dirty. She wore overalls and work boots. Her white hair was in a braid twisted upon the top of her head. Some white loose hair fell over her forehead and down around her face and neck.

Old Mrs. Carlisen took a step closer and looked into Rose's beautiful eyes surrounded by a beautiful face. She had never seen a living person like Rose.

Rose spoke first, saying, "I know you do not know me and you do not want me here. I promise I will not be any trouble." Pal was running around the old woman trying to get her attention. Finally, she bent down and he immediately licked her face. Rose thought she saw a little tenderness on her face.

Rose's Heart's Decision

Old Mrs. Carlisen finally answered, "You'll have to work while you're here."

Old Mrs. Carlisen had no idea who Rose Donlin was.

Chapter 20

Before Toby left, Rose whispered in his ear to, "bring all of my books from Joseph's cabin, also hide my horse for a few days. Then bring him here to the stable."

The room Rose was given was next to the kitchen. The next morning she had the cast iron stove hot and the coffee cooked and ready. The bread was mixed and rising on the back of the stove when the old woman walked into her kitchen. The two women greeted each other coolly and old Mrs. Carlisen gave no recognition of Rose rising earlier or the work she had done.

Rose had not noticed the limp the old woman profusely showed. She sat down at the table and Rose poured her coffee and made her oatmeal. The old woman never looked up but drank her coffee and ate her oatmeal and scraped her bowl clean.

The old woman looked up at Rose and said, "Are you going to marry Toby?"

Rose knew she had to be very careful in her answer because the old woman loved Toby as a son. Before Rose answered, she heard more questions, "Where did you come from? Who have you been living with? Why are you homeless? Do you have any money to help Toby? What are you running from? If you are going to stay here you need to tell me who you are." Old Mrs. Carlisen's eyes were staring at Rose and her voice had become louder with each question. Then she yelled, "When do you plan to marry Toby?"

The knock on the door broke into their thoughts. Then Toby yelled, "It's me, open the door." He had a large wooden box in his arms. Rose's books were piled high in the box.

Rose pointed to her room. Toby returned to the kitchen and touched the old woman in a warm gesture. She looked up at him and the love she felt for him was very evident to Rose.

Toby sensed the problems between the two women would only get worse until he told the old woman the whole story. He had heard the loud conversation when he came to the cabin door.

Rose slipped into her room and closed the door but did not shut it completely. She thought the old woman would ask her to leave when she found out she did not come here to marry Toby.

Rose heard Toby say, "Rose Donlin is here on a mission. She is here to build a hospital and library." Then she heard the old woman say," But do you love her?" Rose had been taking one book out of the wooden box at a time looking for a book with a picture of a large building while listening to Toby and the old woman. Rose instantly stopped and listened. The silence made a shiver run down her spine.

Toby's answer made Rose Donlin gasp.

Old Mrs. Carlisen yelled, "Toby, you must get married now. You and Rose can live here until you have the money to build a cabin."

Suddenly without warning a vision of Henry Helgins appeared to Rose. Tears began to run down her cheeks. He was smiling at her the way he had for the month they had spent together.

With only a few books left in the wooden box, Rose found the book she was looking for.

Rose's door slowly opened and the old woman stood smiling at her. Looking at Rose that way, Rose felt sick to her stomach. Old Mrs Carlisen had not had any happiness since the accident so long ago, until now.

Rose had always smiled easily, but she found it very difficult at this time. Her voice sounded like a whisper, "I need to give this book to Toby," as she slipped by her.

Rose approached Toby with her back to the cabin. She gave Toby the book with the pictures and gave him specific instructions. The length of the building, size of the rooms. She was very firm while telling Toby about the birthing room. She wanted the room free of germs. It had to be clean and sanitary. It had to be wholesome and quiet. Rose stopped and then said, "Where is my horse Toby?"

Toby took a step closer to Rose and lowered his head without looking into her eyes. He began leaning on one foot and kicking the ground with the other. This was when Rose realized something was very wrong.

"Rose, oh god, Rose," Toby began, "I'm so sorry, your horse is gone. I took the big horse home like you asked and the next morning he was gone."

"Toby, by home, by home do you mean your home or Joseph's cabin?" Rose hurriedly asked.

Toby's answer was he had taken her big animal to Joseph's cabin and was not aware the dark-skinned man had been snooping around and had been seen by Rufus George the week before.

Rose wanted to cry but she knew old Mrs. Carlisen was watching from her cabin. She refused to let the old woman see her cry, especially over her horse. But she would not let anyone steal a horse from her.

"Toby," Rose said slowly, "Do you know that a horse thief can be shot without going to jail? You have to get my horse back, Toby."

"Rose," Toby said, with determination in his voice. "I don't have a pistol. I only have a rifle."

Rose took another step closer. She was close enough to kiss him. From the cabin, Old Mrs. Carlisen was watching closely and thinking she was going to see them kiss. Rose said sternly with her teeth clenched hard together, "Toby, I have a pistol. It's in my room at the boarding house in Oklahoma City. It's hidden at the bottom of my satchel."

"Ok Rose, but I'm not sure about shooting someone." Toby said. "Maybe if you could just scare him." Rose said hoping she could convince him to help get the horse back.

Toby was strong. But shooting a man, to him was not anything to take lightly. He told Rose, "I'll come back after dark and take you to the building site." Surprising Rose, he quickly leaned forward and kissed her on the cheek. Nothing could have pleased old Mrs. Carlisen more. She was still smiling when Rose went toward the cabin. She watched as Rose walked swiftly toward the

Rose's Heart's Decision

cabin. Rose was everything a mother would want for her son. A calm, gentle sincere woman. One who would work hard and do as her husband said. Rose spent her day thinking about the hospital and library. Also thinking about where her horse could be. The day seemed to drag by and she stayed away from the old woman as much as she could. They ate supper in silence.

Toby arrived after dark. The old woman agreed a horseback ride would be good for Rose. The horses headed in the direction of the hospital building site. Rose rode along thinking about someone else. But she could tell how Toby was beginning to feel about her. She had not planned on this.

The clouds drifted over the moon, making it hard to see at times. When the sky did light up, Rose was extremely happy at the work done on the hospital. The building was becoming real to her. The walls for the first floor were done. Toby mentioned how all of her renters were working long hours. He also mentioned he had her gun. As he was talking, Rose looked passed him and the movement stopped that she thought she had seen.

Chapter 21

The ride back to old Mrs. Carlisen's cabin felt so emotional, yet agitated, about having to be an imposter. The emotions she felt were over the thought Toby was falling in love with her. The agitation was how she longed to be free. She wanted to be able to watch the hospital and library being built. Hiding her identity from the old woman was immoral and now she was regretting it. It had been a hasty decision to come here. When they got to the stable, Toby helped Rose bed down the horse the old woman had let her use. He told Rose how he informed the men to watch for Rose's horse. He said, "The dark-skinned man is not working at the lumberyard any more. He has been seen riding around town with some pretty tough looking hombres."

"What's he riding on?" Rose asked quickly with eagerness in her voice. "Not your horse, I've asked several men," he answered knowing how upset she was. Feeling uneasy, Rose turned and hurried out of the stable, afraid Toby would reach for her and touch her.

Toby yelled, "Good-night, Rose honey." Rose was relieved as she watched Toby ride toward the road. Overhead the clouds were continuing to gather fiercely. The wind had a chill to it. She felt uneasy entering the cabin. It was so dark. Rose stepped in and closed the door. The voice of the old woman made her jump. She was sitting in the dark as if waiting for Rose.

"You need to marry Toby now." The old woman said in a demanding sound. "You can't be seen alone with a man and not be married to him."

"Toby is building a hospital and library before he can think of marrying anyone," Rose said as she reached her bedroom door, stepped in and closed the door before old Mrs. Carlisen could say more. Rose layed on top of her bed, fully clothed and covered up with a patch quilt. Her deep sleep was needed.

Chapter 22

Noisy sounds were trying to get to Rose so she pulled the quilt up over her head. The pounding on her door and the loud shouting would not stop. Then she felt a hand on her shoulder and her body was being shaken.

Toby was yelling her name and saying, "It's the hospital. It's the hospital. Someone set it on fire. It burned to the ground." Rose Donlin leaped out of bed, trying to come out of a groggy feeling.

Men's angry voices were heard outside all around the cabin. Old Mrs. Carlisen never wanted anyone at her cabin but Toby. She became enraged with anger. Yelling and screaming at the men, "Get out, get off of my property." The men outside were yelling to Rose, "We know who started the fire. It was the dark-skinned man. We have a posse; we're ready to go after him."

Suddenly a shot rang out, and Rose was standing in the front yard with old Mrs. Carlisen's rifle.

"No. No, we'll get him later." No longer was someone else going to run her life. She had to deal with this intruder again. Only this time she had help. "He and his men are probably in Mexico by now," she told them. "He is a fugitive." He had been seen starting the fire. He was wanted in the state of Missouri. Now he was wanted in Oklahoma. "We need to start again. We have to clean up the debris. Go back to the site and clean up the ruins and ashes." Rose pleaded. "Toby, go back to the lumber yard in Oklahoma City, and order all of the boards, windows, and roofing materials. We will work around the clock. At night we will use lanterns. We will guard the grounds," Rose was adamant.

Old Mrs. Carlisen was in a state of shock. She was watching and staring at Rose Donlin, yelling orders to all of the men in her yard.

"Who was this woman?" she thought.

Every renter turned his horse around and headed back to the site. Each man was silent. The last man rode down the lane, and Rose Donlin knew she had to tell the old woman who she really was.

Rose walked to the cabin door and old Mrs. Carlisen was standing in front of the door waiting impatiently.

Rose spoke first. "I'm sorry, Mrs. Carlisen, for not telling you when I first came to your cabin."

"Five and one-half years ago, I was sent here to Oklahoma from the state of Missouri by my father. Joseph Higgins was the man I was sent to. I lived with him and took care of him."

"Did Joseph Higgins die? Were you married to him? Who are you hiding from?" The old woman kept interrupting. "Yes, Mrs. Carlisen, Joseph Higgins died, and left me everything he owned." And then said in a tone of defiance, "No, I was not married to him." With her eyes squinting, and staring at Rose, the old woman opened her mouth and then as if thinking over what Rose had just said, she began yelling, "You own my land and cabin?" Rose answered very slowly, "All of the land that once belonged to the Higgins' family, is now all mine."

The old woman's eyes went from squinting to wide open and she took a step closer to Rose. Rose drew in a deep breath and said, "What is your first name?"

Without any hesitation the old woman said, "Maude."

Rose repeated the name, "Maude."

⌒ Chapter 23 ⌒

"Maude, how did your husband die?"

Maude walked to her rocking chair and started to rock. Then tears welled up in her eyes. Then the sobs came. It was over thirty years of grief. She had been hating herself for all of those years. Rose walked over to the rocking chair and sat down by the old woman's feet.

The story that she had held in came pouring out in a sorrowful, guilt ridden voice. She said, "I killed the only person that ever really loved me and I lost our baby I was carrying. It was all of my fault." Rose interrupted the sobbing woman and said, "What was it you did?" The old woman's wrinkled face was red from crying and the tears kept streaming down her cheeks. Rose asked again, "What was it you did?"

Maude laid her head back and thirty years of carrying a burden with no one to talk to about it came out in painful sounds.

"I shot him, I shot him. He had gotten up to check his mare. She was ready to birth her colt. I did not know he had left the cabin and I heard a noise. Joseph had warned all of his renters of chicken theives. I saw a shadow and I ran for my rifle. I shot at the shadow, and I killed him."

She continued after Rose waited for her to get her air. "I rode to Joseph Higgins' cabin and he took care of everything for me. He brought out the undertaker from Oklahoma City with his essentials. We buried him out behind the cabin in a box Joseph made. I go there every day and tell him how sorry I am."

Maude's tiny body was shaking violently from the shock of hearing her own story said out loud. Rose grabbed a patchwork quilt off of her bed and covered Maude to try and comfort her. Then she lowered herself and was on her knees beside the rocking chair. She gently and sincerely put her arms around the old woman. She held her close and hugged her, and after kissing her forehead, just held her close.

Maude had had no human touch except for Toby. No woman had been to her cabin. She had carried her secret alone. The stories heard in town when the accident happened made Maude look bad. Joseph had been to the law and took care of any threat of an arrest.

While Rose held her she asked, "Maude, how did Toby come to be part of your life?"

In a scratchy voice, Maude told Rose. "Toby was around four years old. He wandered away from home the day we buried my dear husband. We were lowering the box into the ground and I looked up to see a little boy standing there. He sat down on the ground and stayed while Joseph and the undertaker covered the box."

"He was wearing a dirty homemade pair of overalls. His hair was long and I thought he needed care. He was the youngest of a very large family. And I remember wishing he were mine. When Joseph left, he took the boy home. The very next day the little boy returned. He knocked on my door. After I opened the door, he walked right in. He had picked some wildflowers on his way. Toby held them out to me and all I could do was cry." Maude said. "Each day Toby returned. He tried to help me do chores or he would help me plant my garden. My crops were poor the next few years until Toby was big enough to help me with the field work." Maude relaxed and seemed to enjoy talking about Toby. "Now, he does all of my farm work and gets no money. I have no money to give him." Maude said with sadness.

⟶ Chapter 24 ⟵

While holding Maude, Rose hesitated and then said, "Maude, I am going to take care of you. This cabin, and the land Toby farms for you, will be yours. You will never need, or long for or want.

Rose became aware Maude's body relaxed almost limp in her arms. She helped the old woman into her bedroom and laid her on her bed, then covered her. Maude's breathing changed and her much needed sleep was extremely peaceful. She had released the hate for herself that she had harbored most of her life. Rose's night was without sleep. Leaving her and abandoning the old woman now with Toby so busy building the hospital, would only continue her previous lonely non-existant life, and also taking Pal away from her now that they had become friends. Rose had witnessed many times the gentle playful times they had together. Maude was still penniless after living frugally all of her life. The only thing she owned was her one horse. Maude slept soundly all evening and into the night.

The following morning, Rose made it very clear to her. "Maude, you must listen to me," said Rose sternly. " It was an accident, where no one is to blame. No one is to take the blame, you are not guilty of killing your husband on purpose. You must stop blaming yourself."

Maude sat silently listening, wanting the guilt to leave her mind. Toby knocked once and walked into the cabin. Rose and Maude looked up into a face that was tired and frowning. Rose was on her feet saying, "Oh, Toby, what's wrong?"

"Rose, someone is shooting at your renters while they're working on the hospital. They're really getting scared. Some of them are not showing up to work. The shooter shows up at sundown and stays off in the distance. We think we know who it is. The horse he rides can outrun any one that chases him."

"Toby," Rose said, with anger in her voice. "Is it him? Is he riding the horse?" Maude sounded loud and stern, when she looked at Rose and said, "Rose, is this the man you're hiding from?"

"Yes, yes. I'm sure it's him. The reason he can out run any other horse is because he's riding the most magnificent horse in the state. No one can catch him." Rose answered Maude.

Maude spoke directly to Toby. "If he shows up at dark, gather all of the men into the shelter of the hospital and you can use my rifle. It can hit anything within a half a mile."

"Please, Toby, make sure you don't hit the horse, please," Rose begged. "Toby, when you aim my rifle, make sure you're ready to take a man's life, because I know what it's like to live in regret," Maude told him.

"No wait, I'll do it. I'm the one to do it. That man is after me," said Rose walking to where the rifle was hanging over the fireplace. Toby and Maude stood in silence, watching her take the large rifle down. Maude's voice was almost a whisper saying, "It's loaded Rose." Toby moved toward the door. When he opened the door, Rose said, "Tell all of the men that I'll come when the sun goes down."

Rose tried to put the idea of having to shoot a man out of her mind, but the picture kept creeping back. Maude told Rose she could use Toby's rifle and if they both shot at the same time no one would know which bullet hit the darkskinned man. Rose refused to let Maude shoot another man.

Rose was surprised Maude was willing to leave her homestead. She had not left it for thirty years but Toby was involved, and she would do anything to protect him.

It was nearly dark when Maude headed for her stable with Rose walking behind. Maude's horse would have to carry them both to the hospital site. The stars were all covered with dark angry looking clouds. They both rode in silence with their own thoughts.

Before Rose and Maude reached their destination the lightning was streaking viciously all across the sky. Then the dark clouds crashed into one another with so much force, the sounds were deafening and terrifying. Maude's horse was jumping and throwing his head up at the clap of thunder, making it difficult to hold on.

The lightning made it easy to ride up close to the building. No lanterns were lit. Rose slipped off of the back of the horse and waited for Maude to get off of the saddle. With no hesitation she grabbed the reins from Maude and tried to get into the saddle. It took three tries. The horse was wild, moving away from Rose in a circle. After she got into the saddle, Maude handed her the rifle.

Rose had no idea which direction to ride in. The horse wanted to run, and the direction didn't matter to him. He began to jump and run. The lightning and thunder were closer and now the rain was coming in a violent stream. Rose was not wearing her hat. The rain was rapidly running down her face and into her eyes making it hard to see. The next streak of lightning, Rose found herself within 500 feet of a man on a giant horse. In an instant Rose raised Maude's rifle to shoot at a man and take his life. She waited for the next lightning to pull the trigger. Suddenly a red streak missed her. The man had just shot at her. The lightning again lit up and Rose witnessed flashes coming from another direction. Then she realized someone else was shooting at the man on the horse. Several horses rode toward the man.

Chapter 25

Rose sat in the pouring rain not understanding what had just happened. Then she thought she heard someone call out her name. It was Toby.

"Toby, Toby, what are you doing here?"asked Rose.

"Rose," Toby hollered back, "I asked the sheriff for help, he and his men shot the man on your horse."

"Oh Toby, is he, is the man dead?" asked Rose.

"I don't know Rose," said Toby. "The sheriff took him and your horse back into town. I'll get your horse tomorrow. I promise." Toby moved his horse up to Rose as close as he could. He reached out in spite of the constant powerful rain, and touched her arm.

"Rose," Toby said, slowly and softly. "You look so beautiful in the rain. I, I."

"Toby," Rose cried out to stop him from saying what she thought he was going to say. "Toby, there is someone else." Rose said, with a very empty feeling in her heart. "I am truly sorry."

"But where is he?" Toby was not going to give up. "How come I haven't seen him, Rose?"

"Toby, listen, he went home to his family, to help his family." "If you were my girl, I sure wouldn't leave you." Toby came back more determined than before.

Rose was so relieved Toby could not see the tears starting to flow down with the rain on her face. Toby was a good man. If he was going to pursue her, she would have to find Henry Helgens sooner than she had planned.

Rose pulled on the reins to start back to the hospital site. Toby rode as close as he could. Giving up Rose was not going to be easy for him.

Chapter 26

The sound of hammers pounding grew louder as they approached the new building. The lanterns were all lit as Rose and Toby stepped through the door. The men were all working on the inside. The rooms had been all measured off.

Word of the shooting had been told to the men. Everything had quickly changed. The men were talking

and laughing as before. Rufus George showed no fear. He
carried the heavy lumber and he could reach up higher
to pound in nails than any other man. Rose watched the
men respond to him. If he did not understand, the men
took time to explain what he needed to do.

Maude was completely stunned when she first looked
at Rufus George. She had lived her entire life with no
knowledge people like Rufus George existed. She moved
over into a dark corner to watch this huge man. In her
hands she held her rifle taken from Rose. The only sound
coming from the corner she stood in was her heavy
breathing.

Maude raised her rifle. In the darkness, she tried
to aim her gun at the black man. The shadows darted
around the room. She moved the rifle to one man and
aimed. Then the light showed him to be a white man.
She jerked the rifle to the next man. His shadow covered
one wall while reaching to the ceiling. The lantern light
shined on Rufus George. All Maude could see was the
white of his eyes.

With her finger on the trigger, Maude hesitated for a split second, giving Rose time to grab her arm and Toby grabbed the rifle.

For the next few minutes Toby spent time explaining what a great man Rufus George was. Toby told her the color on the outside of a man is not what is important, it's what is in his heart.

Rose needed to get Maude back to her cabin to rest and get her dry clothes before another accident happened. The rain had eased up for the ride home. Maude was quiet on the ride. She was not sure her mind was clear, thinking of a man whose skin was black. Did she really see this man?

Chapter 27

Rose left Maude off at the door of her cabin and told her to get out of her wet clothes. She also told her to hang them next to the fire place to dry. Rose fed and bedded the horse down.

Rose had breakfast ready the next morning and was waiting for Maude when she heard a tap on the door. The door opened and Toby stepped in. His intensive stare told Rose he had something on his mind.

"Rose, I went into town early this morning to talk to the sheriff about your horse," Toby stopped and then said, "You have to prove the horse is yours." "But, Toby, I don't have any proof at all," Rose admitted. "I just claimed him as my own."

Maude walked into the room looking her age, but she looked clean from the rain and her hair had been combed. She paused before sitting down next to Toby after hearing his conversation with Rose and said, "Rose, go into town and tell the sheriff, the horse was always yours. Tell him the darkskinned man stole him from you and ask the stable hand to tell the sheriff he had been taking care of the horse for you."

Rose was listening and eating her oatmeal. Then she heard Toby say, "Rose, I have one more thing to tell you. There are more oil spots appearing on the ground around your homestead. Also I lifted the cave door and the oil is up to the second step." Toby and Maude sat quietly waiting for Rose to answer. At that minute Rose was remembering what Joseph had told her when she finally told him she had seen the oil bubbling up out of the ground. Joseph had said, "The big machines will come and dig up my land. When the time is right, I will pump the oil up." Rose looked up and answered Toby by saying, "The hospital must be finished first and then I'll pump out the oil. After that, we'll build the library."

⤳ Chapter 28 ⤶

"Now I need to go into Oklahoma City to bring my horse here,"said Rose. "Maude, I would like you to go with me." Toby left to get Maude's horse ready for the trip into town. Maude crawled up into the saddle, and Rose rode behind the saddle. The ride took nearly an hour. Rose directed Maude to the livery stable. The stable was quiet as no horse was in sight. Rose suddenly felt uneasy. Then she thought she heard a noise as if someone was moaning Maude found the stable hand first. He had bruises on his face. While Maude talked to the man, Rose hurried to the back of the stable where the large horse had always been kept. Rose returned to the front stall and questioned the shaken man. He told her, "Someone snuck up from behind and hit me hard." At first he did not know the big horse was gone. The welt sticking out on the back of his head told Rose he was telling the truth.

Rose yelled, "Let's go Maude." The sheriff"s office was across town and Maude's horse galloped all of the way. The news from the sheriff was not the news Rose wanted to hear. The sheriff said, "The darkskinned man was shot by one of my men. We brought him into town to see a doctor and as soon as the doctor took the bullet out, he escaped."

Maude looked over at Rose while hearing her say, "Oh no, he escaped? How could you let this happen?" The sheriff did not answer the question. The look on his face told Rose he was not going to.

"Rose Donlin, this man is very dangerous. You must be extremely careful. If he has not left the area, according to what my men are telling me, you are who he wants."

Maude jumped to her feet first. Her voice was high pitched and squeaky, "You listen to me sheriff. If something happens to this young woman, you're going to be punished the rest of your life," then paused, "by me." Without even knowing the old woman, the sheriff could tell he should believe what she was saying.

He had an answer and he stated it so Rose and Maude could understand it. His eyes darted from one to the other. Then began in a strong sounding voice, "First, I do want to protect you. But, the only way is for you to stay here in a jail cell. Rose, I cannot protect you if you go out on the street."

 Chapter 29

Rose stood up slowly and walked to the window. She gazed out at the busy street. She thought how fast Oklahoma City had grown in the five and one-half years since she had stepped off of the train. She noticed more stores had opened up. The large glass windows showed beautiful dresses and suits like John Fitzpatrick wore. Then her eyes rested on the bank and especially the sign out in front. Higgins and Fitzpatrick. She recognized John Fitzpatrick standing behind the counter. He was dressed in a black suit as usual.

Rose seemed transfixed in her own memories.

John had been part of her life while she lived with Joseph Higgins, but the meeting John had with Rufus George in the cabin was what came into her mind. What Rose wanted to remember were the trips John made to the cabin when she thought she could be in love with him. The vision of Rufus George standing with his hand out and John refusing to shake it was a disappointment and very hurtful for her. Rose wondered why John Fitzpatrick acted so harshly because surely he knew slavery was over. She decided she could not ask him for help like she had done when Joseph died. Was this the time to send a telegram?

Maude slipped up beside Rose. She looked out of the window in the area Rose was looking. The sign over the bank caught her eye. Higgins and Fitzpatrick. Maude leaned over and whispered in Rose's ear, "Joseph's last name was Higgins."

Rose's voice was soft in her answer,"Yes."

Maude was aware how sad Rose was feeling, she could hear it in her voice. Rose's shoulders slumped forward and her face looked pale and colorless.

Maude gently took hold of Rose's arm and said, "Lets go home to my cabin. I'll watch over you." Then she raised her voice and said, "I'll shoot the first man that comes near us."

The sheriff had been listening and when he heard Maude, he was furious. "No, you cannot shoot anyone because you will be arrested." Maude's instant reply was, "Then, do your job and capture this man."

Rose did not give the sheriff time to answer. She said, "About the horse. The horse belongs to me. The man took it; he stole my horse. Talk to the man that works at the stable."

Chapter 30

Rose walked out onto the street and let the fresh air blow against her beautiful sweet flawless face. Maude's steps were right behind her and Rose knew she was safe. The old woman was fearless, high spirited and persistent.

Rose stopped abruptly, and Maude bumped into her. Rose heard her name being called from across the street. She turned only for a second and recognized John Fitzpatrick standing in front of the bank.

This was the moment Rose needed to wash away any doubt she had of releasing John from her past dreams of marrying him. The whole world disappeared and they could see no one else but each other. Rose visioned John and Henry Helgens standing side by side. And then her heart made the decision. She slowly turned away.

The bright sun felt warm even with a chill in the air. Maude's horse was standing in the same spot not having to be tied up. Domesticated and patient, nothing like his owner.

The ride to the boarding house took only a few minutes. Rose explained to Maude they would stay in her room for the night. "In the morning," Rose went on to say, "I need to send a telegram to a friend."

Maude's horse would have to stand in the alley behind the boarding house after Rose removed the saddle. She carried the saddle into the boarding house basement.

In the room that night Maude questioned Rose about her life. Maude always ended each sentence with what a good man Toby was.

Maude insisted on going to the telegraph office with Rose. The young man was surprised and glad to see the lovely young woman again. Maude stood so close to Rose she could feel Maude's warm breath on her neck. It suddenly appeared to Rose, Maude wanted to know everything about her and she wanted to keep every young man away from her except one, Toby.

Rose did not have to be told what a good man Toby was. But Henry Helgens was a very good man too.

Rose turned her back on Maude while she cautiously grabbed a piece of paper and pencil. She wrote four words."Please Come, Rose Donlin." Rose folded the paper tightly and quickly handed it to the young man before Maude could read it.

Rose said, "Send this to Henry Helgens." She then left the office with Maude nearly walking on her heals.

"Who is Henry Helgens, Rose?" Maude sounded determined to know. "A friend." Rose answered. "Just a friend."

The ride toward Maude's cabin was the second stop. The first stop was to the Higgins hospital. It was nearly complete. Toby greeted them both with a huge smile. Rose was totally surprised at her own reaction to seeing him. Her response was a smile and wave. She told herself it was because of the beautiful building.

Maude was watching them both and she tried to hide any happiness she felt.

Rufus George was busy unloading a wagon full of bed frames. Also large boxes of bedding materials. He stopped long enough to greet Rose and Maude. Maude stepped behind Rose with a bewildered look of uncertainty.

Rose shook hands with Rufus George and thanked him over and over for all he had done for her. He had worked endless hours doing what he enjoyed, just working.

Maude watched this giant man being so gentle with Rose. Maude leaned out from behind Rose and reached out her hand with her arm fully extended. Rufus George could see only an aged wrinkled hand. He graciously touched her hand. And then through the stillness, Rufus George said, "Me aar appy to be shakkin in you lif."

Toby stood staring in complete disbelief of what he had just seen and heard. Rose was as adamant about helping the downtrodden man as Maude had been unyielding when she first saw him.

Chapter 31

Toby offered to accompany Rose and Maude back to her cabin. Rose insisted they were capable of getting to Maude's cabin safely. Rose informed Toby he was needed to finish the work on the hospital. The ride was quiet except for Maude's horse's hooves making a rythmic sound. The sky was filled with stars that glistened like diamonds. The night air felt cool with only a small breeze.

They were within a mile of the cabin when Rose whispered in Maude's ear, "I think I hear another horse." Maude pulled back on her horse's reins to stop him. Maude whispered, "I hear it too." Slowly Maude pulled out her rifle from its leather holder. She quietly put her heel into each side of her horse and pulled on one rein and the horse moved off of the trail into a wooded area.

Maude stopped her horse. Shadows from the trees and limbs were giantic in size.

The night sounds of the wooded area could not drown out the horse's hooves coming closer. Maude and Rose sat as quietly as they could. Rose's hand reached down and unhooked the lasso from the saddle. She knew she had to do something and now was the time.

Rose told Maude exactly what they had to do. They both slipped off of Maude's horse and stepped softly to the tree next to the trail. Rose tied one end around the top of a tree trunk and then as quietly as she could, tied the other end on the trunk of a tree on the opposite side of the trail.

Then Rose and Maude waited. Rose stood next to one tree and Maude stood next to the rope on the other side. Rose determined the man was riding on a rather large horse as the sound of the hooves was loud.

It happened fast. It was a complete surprise, and Rose saw the man fall backward off of the giant horse. Each of the rope ends were untied from the trees and before the man could move, Rose and Maude had him tied securely so he could not even move a finger.

The dark skinned man was horrified at what had just happened and that it was done by two women. His immediate reaction was twisting and turning while jerking against the ropes. He tried to loosen the rope to get free. The darkness prevented him from seeing the women's faces but he had heard their voices. Nothing could have brought on his rage more.

Maude had never heard swear words in Spanish before like the man was yelling and screaming at she and Rose. Before lifting him up onto the back of Maude's horse, the women used his own hankerchief and tied it over his mouth and around his head.

It took several tries before they could get him up and laid across the horse. Then Rose unsnapped one of the reins from the bridle and slipped one end through the rope to secure the man to the saddle. Falling off in the dark could let him escape again.

Standing next to the giant horse made Rose extremely happy. She felt only love and security as she laid her face up against his neck. Rose whispered, "I've missed you so."

$\sim$ Chapter 32 $\sim$

The large horse stood patiently waiting for both Rose and Maude to get upon him. Rose had a rein from Maude's horse in her hand. The horse was led close behind the large horse. Rose sat behind Maude and turned frequently to watch the dark skinned man. The mile left to ride was needed for Rose to decide where she would keep the man until Toby returned.

Rose planned to ask Toby to take the man back into town and take him directly to the sheriff"s office. Maude looked straight ahead, but whispered to Rose, "I have an idea, we can put him in my grain bin. All I have to do is fix the lock on the door."

"Maude," Rose whispered back, "Are you sure he can't get out?"

"Yes, I'll make sure of it," Maude said reassuringly. After they reached Maude's cabin, she lit a lantern while Rose led the horse with the man tied to the saddle up to the grain bin. It was planned how they would get the man off of the horse and drug into the grain bin. Once inside they stood him up and tied ropes around each wrist with his hands already tied behind his back. They worked the ends of each rope between the boards up over his head. When Rose loosened his hands they each pulled his hands up and out to the side of him and secured the ropes. He was standing up with his arms and hands tied and then they tied his ankles to the boards. He tried hard to move but the ropes would not give at all. They both stood back and looked at the man and Rose said, "Do you have more rope, Maude?" The rope Maude brought from the barn was wrapped around him and tied. He could not move.

Rose said, "I'll stay out here with him."

"My rifle is loaded," Maude said as she handed it to Rose. The hankerchief remained tied over his mouth. With the lantern light, Rose could see his eyes were fixed on her and he continued to glare at her. The frown made wrinkles all over his face. Rose thought she could feel the hate radiating off of him. He would never let her go if he got loose. Rose moved slowly to the door. The light from the lantern in her hand began to darken the grain bin. The sound the man made, coming out through the hankerchief was an evil savage gruesome outburst. She closed the door. The lock was put in place. To save the kerosene in the lantern Rose turned the wick down as far as she could.

Maude had placed a gunny sack on the ground outside of the bin for Rose to sit on. The noise from the grain bin stopped when he had exhausted his energy. The night reminded her of the day and night she laid under a large fallen tree. It was after the darkskinned man kidnapped her from the train. At that time she was frightened, alone and she was still feeling the fear of this man as she was then. Rose closed her eyes and tried to block out the man's wicked eyes from her mind. She hoped Toby came early in the morning. The man had not had anything to eat or drink. The night's events were catching up with her and Rose was feeling cold and tired. Her eyes were heavy and she wanted to sleep. From the distance of the barn Rose could hear the two horses moving about or stomping their feet on the floor boards. She could also hear them eating the hay from the manger.

⌒ᵔ Chapter 33 ᵔ⌒

Then without any knowledge of someone coming, a hand was over her mouth. The other arm was around her, holding her so tight she could not get away as she was being lifted up to her feet. She jerked one way and then another. Rose lifted her leg and with her foot and toes pointing downward she kicked backwards and struck a leg. She heard a man's moan and then they both fell to the ground. He did not loosen his hold on her, he was laying on top of her.

While his head was next to hers, he said, "Rose, Rose, it's me, Toby. The man's men are coming, they know he's here. We have to move him to a better hiding place. I could hear him mumbling when I came here so they will know where he is. "Rose felt relief, but her anger and terrified fright made her want to lash out at Toby. She wanted to cough from the feeling of being choked. But she knew any noise would be heard by the darkskinned man's men. Toby told her he was afraid she would shoot him. He went on to whisper, that, "Pal is in the cave with Maude. We have to hurry, Rose." Rose unlocked the grain bin door then she turned the lantern off.

Toby had been in the grain bin many times, so he was very familier within it. While Toby quickly pulled the ropes out of the boards up over the man's head. The man slumped to the floor, for he had been hanging with his feet off of the bin floor because Rose and Maude had pulled the ropes so tightly. Toby carried the man out into the night air and continued hurrying in the direction of an abandoned well. Rose was following a few steps behind.

The rope in the well remained intact wound around the wooden bucket. Toby asked Rose to untie the rope from the water bucket. Toby grabbed the well rope from Rose and tied it around and under the arms of the dark skinned man. He then lifted him over and down into the dark deep well and took the crank that Rose was holding and Toby unwound the rope until he had the man lowered to the bottom and stopped before his feet could touch the dry dirt.

Toby reached out in the dark grabbing Rose's arm and all he said was, "This way." He drug and pushed her as they stumbled along toward the back of the cabin. Toby stopped and lifted up the door of the cave. Rose could hear Pal jumping around in the cave as Maude tried to hold him to keep him quiet. Toby entered first and reached back for Rose. As soon as they were in the cave, Toby leaned back and closed the cave door.

Chapter 34

Total darkness surrounded them in the damp musty odor of the cave. Within minutes in the darkness they all heard strange noises. Then they felt the ground above them vibrate and dirt clods were falling on them and breaking off on the sides of the cave. The air in the cave was suddenly full of dust and each one wanted to cough and climb up out of this dark dank underground room, "the cave." Pal was almost uncontrollable.

The horses continued moving around over their heads. They could hear the snorting of the horses as the air went in and out of their noses. The noise, from the creaking of the saddles, was loud in the cave. The brutal sound of the horses being slapped with the reins made them all cringe. The dirt and dust continued to engulf them. Then suddenly the ground above them stopped vibrating and the dirt stopped falling in on them.

Toby lifted the cave door only a few inches. The horses had left. He needed to get every one up and out for air. Maude came up next and put her hand out for Rose to take. Toby ran in the dark to the well. The dark-skinned man's men had not found him.

Maude guided Rose into the cabin and filled the fireplace to warm the cold cabin. Toby stepped into the cabin and told Rose the man was still in the well and at the break of dawn he would take him into town and turn him over to the sheriff. Rose yelled at Toby to check her horse. He smiled at her with his face covered with dirt and squinting through heavy eyes, his face lit up and he said, "I took care of your horse last night. I took him into the wooden area out behind Maude's barn. He's tied to a tree." Rose sat down at Maude's table and laid her head on her folded arms and tried to hide her feelings of gratefulness because she wondered if it was more and she was becoming dependent on him. And she did not want to.

Chapter 35

Each one took turns dipping water out of the water pail and into the basin to wash off the dirt. Pal had shaken the dust and dirt off when he ran up the steps and out of the cave. He lay near the door watching as Maude, Rose and Toby cleaned off their dirt.

Pal was laying on his stomach with his front legs extended out. His head rested on the floor with his eyes closed. Maude had fed him milk with bread soaked in it. He was warm and tired from the night in the cave. His lips moved in rhythm as he breathed in and out in his sleep. No one but Pal heard the noise. He stood up as if in slow motion. Straight up on his feet. His head towered over his body and both ears up as he was listening. Pal made the turn toward the door fast. His nose was up against the door. The hair stood up from the top of his neck to his tail. And then he began to growl. A deep warning growl. Someone was outside of the cabin.

Maude reached for her rifle over the fireplace and moved immediately to the door. Toby stepped over in front of Rose. He reached back and with one arm brought her up close to his back. Toby's strong arm remained around her making it impossible for Rose to move. She was pressed up against his broad firm muscular back. She tried to take a deep breath but could only manage little breaths. No one said a word inside the cabin. They all remained silent.

Then from outside they heard a loud voice say, "This is the sheriff, is everyone ok in there?" He stopped walking toward the cabin when he saw a small amount of light coming from the small open space of the door. He could see a tiny figure, but what he noticed more was the shot gun the tiny figure was holding. The two barrels would not miss his stomach.

Maude's eye's were searching frantically for a star badge on the man's coat. When she caught a glimpse of it she slowly lowered her gun. Toby opened the door and asked the sheriff to, "Come on in."

 Chapter 36

The sheriff accepted the invitation to come in and sat his heavy body down in relief. His body covered the entire chair. In his office he had not appeared oversized, but Maude's cabin was small. He was sitting close to the fireplace with a large riding coat on and he wore a big rimmed cowboy hat. His rawhide gloves looked larger than his hands. Maude's fireplace was hot from burning logs.

Rose sat down across from him. He looked directly at her. She thought he seemed uncomfortable and then she noticed sweat beads coming down on the sides of his face. In the lamp light she could see his eyebrows were long and bushy and when he talked they went up and down as he expressed his words. His hair stuck out from under his hat all around his head. This was definitely not a social call. Maude poured a tin cup full of coffee for him. He could see the steam coming from the cup and decided to talk while the coffee cooled.

He spoke in a slow destinctive loud voice. "I came out to see if everyone was all right here. And also to make sure no one gets hurt. After I talked to you ladies, I thought I needed to warn you the same man my men shot has been seen near here." The sheriff talked slowly while taking sips of coffee. He went on to say, "I need to warn you if you see him, don't try to capture him. He's dangerous and I want to take him alive and unharmed. The person or persons who harm him," the sheriff paused and then said, "Well, I will have to lock up." No one answered the sheriff. Each one hoped he would leave soon.

Rose did not offer him a second cup of coffee. The sheriff picked his cup up and drank the last drop. As he picked the cup up and tipped it over his mouth with his head back, Rose, Maude, and Toby looked quickly at each other and no one spoke. The sheriff pushed his chair back and stood up slowly. He reached the door, took hold of the handle and opened the door then he turned around and spoke in his hardened drawl. "Just remember what I said. Someone will be arrested if that man gets hurt or killed by anyone but one of my men."

Chapter 37

The sheriff rode back into town thinking the three people in the cabin knew something they didn't tell him. He would go to his office and wait. He had made the trip out to Maude's because earlier someone had told him they had seen the dark skinned man riding out of town toward Maude's cabin. And the man was riding on the magnificent horse. Now he had disappeared.

Toby knew what he had to do as fast as he could. He reached the abandoned well. Maude tried to keep up with him. She was only a few steps behind as Toby began to turn the crank winding the rope and bringing the dark skinned man up out of the well.

As soon as Maude could grab onto the man, she tugged and pulled until she could get his feet out and over the well frame. The first thing Maude noticed was his head was limp lying on his chest as was the rest of his body. They laid him on the ground and while Toby untied him, Maude felt his skin. He was cold and damp and his breathing was short and shallow. The sun was up and the sky was clear of any clouds. The fear of being seen by any travelers made them hurry more. Toby picked the man up and lifted the motionless body over his shoulder.

Pal began barking as soon as he heard footsteps coming close to the cabin. Rose stood behind the door as she opened it. Once inside Toby told Rose to stay clear of the man. He told her, "Maude and I will care for him."

Toby shouted orders to Rose and Maude. They did everything he asked. The fireplace was filled with wood.

Coffee was hot. Toby told Rose to get the warmest patchwork quilt she could find. The quilt was put as close as it could be to the fireplace to warm the man's body. Toby wrapped the man up. Then Toby asked Maude for warm wet rags to lay on the man's head and face.

Toby worked on the man rubbing his hands. Replacing the wet warm rags frequently. Then he lifted the man's head and slowly poured sips of hot coffee into his mouth.

The hours slipped by as Toby and Maude tried to save the man's life. Toby insisted Rose not come near the man. He did not want the man to see her.

With the man's eyes still closed, Toby fed him mushy oatmeal and continued with the sips of hot coffee. It was late in the day when the man made a sound. He began to moan and move a little on the quilt.

Chapter 38

Pal had been left out of the cabin to run as he did every day. He heard a horse off in the distance and began to bark. Rose rushed to the door and stood watching Pal as he excitedly ran to the road and back to the cabin barking loudly. No one would be allowed in the cabin today. No one.

The sun was bright and it was shining in Rose's eyes making it difficult to look at the man riding toward her without squinting. The rider was close enough now for Rose to see how he sat straight in his saddle. He was wearing an old worn out cowboy hat but he wore it proudly. The coat he was wearing was a homemade buckskin with fringe hanging from it. He sat holding the reins in one hand. The other hand lay leisurely on his leg. She could see saddlebags laying across the horse's flank behind the saddle, also a large rolledup sleeping bag.

Rose stood watching as the horse came closer. The sun was warm but she suddenly felt cold. Her body began to tremble and she did not know why.

The horse stopped at the end of Maude's lane. He dismounted slow and easy, like a royal horseman. He walked out in front of his horse and stood looking at Rose. He removed his hat and she watched his beautiful curly hair fall down on his forehead.

Rose took one step and stopped. She wanted to let him know how she felt, but she did not know how. Then the steps she took were fast and she raised her arms around Henry Helgens' neck and all the dreaming and longing came out. She opened her mouth slightly and responded to his kiss. Rose kissed him over and over and then leaned up against his body with hers. She laid her head on his shoulder. Out of the corner of her eye she could see Toby standing in the door of Maude's cabin watching.

Tears welled up in Rose's eyes. Henry Helgens' eyes darted from Rose to Toby. Then Toby disappeared back into the cabin. She knew she had to tell Henry everything.

The next hour, she told Henry about going to Joseph's cabin and finding Rufus George. Then meeting Toby and Maude. Now, she had to explain why the darkskinned man was in Maude's cabin and where he was when he nearly died. He needed to know the sheriff came to Maude's cabin. Also the warning the sheriff had stated firmly before he left.

Chapter 39

Rose took Henry's hand and they stepped into the cabin. The cabin was so hot it was almost unbearable. Maude and Toby looked over to see the worry on Rose's face. Rose started to speak, "This is" before she could say Henry's name. Toby interupted her and said, "Help me lift this man onto a chair." Toby was looking directly at Henry.

Henry Helgens moved over and bent down on one side of the man. With Toby on the other side slipping his arm under and around the man. They lifted him easily into one of Maude's chairs. He began to kick and tried to get loose. The words the man spoke were vulgar and mostly Spanish. Toby proceeded to tie the man securely in the chair.

Henry knew exactly who this dark skinned man was. He remembered him coming to his parents cabin in Missouri asking and looking for Rose Donlin.

Rose stood back away from everyone and watched. She could see the quick stares between the two men. Maude looked at each of the men and then over to Rose. The cabin was full of silence.

Rose was sure Toby was hot from the heat coming from the fireplace and tired from the long night. He had tried so hard to save the life of an ungrateful man. And now he was determined to stop Henry from coming into their life and taking Rose away from him.

Maude's voice was loud and clear, "We need to get this man into the sheriff's office now. Keep him tied up until you get to the edge of town. Then untie the rope from around his arms and tie only his hands to the saddle

horn. You," and she looked at Henry," You ride shot gun."
She handed her large rifle to Henry.

As Toby and Henry dragged the man out of the
cabin, both men glanced over at Rose standing back in
the corner of the cabin. Toby had the man's arms tied
closely to his body. Henry lifted the man up on Toby's
horse and he then tied the man's hands around the saddle
horn. Henry spoke to the man in a low voice, "You are
not going to hurt anyone ever again."

When Toby and Henry were out of sight Rose ran
into the trees to find her horse. She found it exactly
where Toby had left it. Maude was waiting for her when
she got back to the lane. Together they rode side by side
into Oklahoma City, out of sight but behind Toby and
Henry.

Chapter 40

It was nearly dark when Rose and Maude rode down
Main Street. The street lamps were all lit. Some of the
merchants' stores were closed for the night. Others had
their lamps shining in the window. One window was dec-
orated so beautifully. On a mannequin, next to the glass
was the most beautiful wedding dress Rose had ever seen.
She hoped Maude was not watching her.

Rose recognized Toby and Henry's horses standing
outside of the sheriff's office. She wanted to go right
in and tell the sheriff to lock the darkskinned man up.
Maude's hand reached over and grabbed one of the reins
from Rose. Maude did not want the sheriff to see she or
Rose. If the man told his story of what happened to him,
he would have no proof. The sheriff's office door opened
up and Toby walked out alone. He looked in Roses direc-

tion, tipped his hat at her and strolled up to and mounted his horse and then rode off toward his home.

Maude quietly backed her horse up into the street and followed Toby out of town.

Rose was left alone feeling impatient and excited waiting for the sheriff's door to open again.

Rose could see the door latch move slowly. She watched Henry step out. He walked to his horse and unwrapped the reins. She continued watching as he turned his horse around and stepped out onto the street. Henry lifted his head up and looked across the street. He couldn't move. Rose was standing under the lamp light She was not wearing a beautiful dress like the one she had seen in the window earlier. And she was not wearing top boots with laces and she was not holding a parasol.

Rose had on an old worn out pair of Maude's overalls and her shirt was a faded chambrey. Her boots were a pair of Toby's. Her light colored hair now hung below her shoulders. The light from the street lamp made it glisten. To Henry, she was more beautiful than any woman he had ever seen. They walked toward each other and out into the middle of the street. She stood so close to him, and then laid her face up against his chest and he rested his chin on her forehead. Rose could feel his warm breath on her face. She felt his arms encircle her. This was how she had dreamed love would be. The comfort of strong arms around her. Knowing she would never be alone again.

Henry whispered in her ear how very much he loved and how much he had missed her. Rose let his words remain in her mind. She wanted this time to last her a life time. Someone shouting from a bar brought them both back to now.

Rose mentioned she had a room at the boarding house. Henry told her he would stay in the livery stable with the horses. "Rose, I have no money. When I received your message, I left home in a hurry. I have only enough to pay to keep my horse over night."

"No," Rose said. "You can use my father's room, I have the key." The light was dim where they stood but Rose could see the questioning look on Henry's face. He still did not know the amount of wealth that was hers.

They led the horses into the stable. The stable hand mentioned it was good to see she had her horse back. Walking back to the boarding house, the streets were quiet except the noises from the horses tied to the hitching post. Talking and laughing could be heard coming from inside of a bar.

Chapter 41

Rose enjoyed the walk to the boarding house because Henry held her hand. When they reached the room she gave the key to him. Rose kissed his cheek and went to open her door. She took a couple of steps and then heard him say, "Rose, I brought someone with me." Before she could say a word. Henry continued, asking, "Do you remember Mary Rocker and her daughters?" He let her answer. "Yes, of course I do. Did you bring Mary here? Where did you find her? Did her daughters come with her? Henry, where are they?" Rose asked question after question. "Rose, do you remember the night we stopped there? Mary begged us to take her with us. I was afraid her husband would hurt her or one of the girls or perhaps you. He had been drinking that day. I told her I would come back and get her. I stopped at their homestead and Jesse was drunk. Mary and the girls were so scared of him. The girls were hiding while Mary did all of the work. Jesse passed out around midnight. I hitched my horse to his buggy using his harness. I put my saddle in the back of the buggy. Mary and the girls came with only the clothes they were wearing. Mary cried most of the way, she was so happy to get away, and most of all her girls were safe. I spent my last dollars to pay for their rooms here in the boarding house."

Rose kissed him again and thanked him, expressing her gratitude. She also told him, "I'll take care of them."

It was nearly noon the following day when Henry heard a light tap on his door. He dressed in a hurry and opened the door to find his beautiful Rose standing there. She asked if he would go to the hospital site with her after they ate dinner at the boarding house diner. With no hesitation he agreed.

Henry and Rose stepped out into the hall. They found Mary and the girls ready to knock on Henry's door. Mary stood with an arm around each girl. A mother alone with no way to feed or clothe her daughters.

Henry had not told them about Rose; only that the person that had been with him the night he had stopped and ate was waiting in Oklahoma City for him.

Rose was not wearing the old hat pulled down tightly over her head and forehead that she wore the night she had met them, to conceal that she was a girl.

Mary's older daughter, Elizabeth, spoke first as she gazed up at Rose. "You do look like a girl. Your hair is long, and your body is," Mary did not give her time to finish what she imagined her daughter was going to say. "You are so beautiful," Mary said.

Henry's laughter filled the hallway. He put his arm around her and told them, "This is my lady, Rose Donlin."

While they ate lunch, Rose told Mary she would purchase all their food and clothing for them. Henry sat silently wondering how Rose planned to do this.

Chapter 42

Long before they reached the hospital Rose could see and marveled at the beautiful outline of the long awaited structure. It was high and straight in the air. The many rooms would bring comfort to the sick.

The big bold letters of the name Higgins were a welcome sight, as were all of the street lamps Toby had ordered. The renters work was completed and they had all left to prepare for spring planting. Rose needed to thank each family and tell them they would not have to pay rent this year for all of the devoted work they had done for her.

Henry had ridden in silence. He remembered the first time Rose told him she planned to build a hospital and library. He had wondered then, as he was wondering now how a young women could do this.

Rose recognized the horse tied to the hitching post behind the hospital. It was Toby's. Along side of Toby's horse was a buckboard and two horses standing patiently waiting. She knew Rufus George was here. The horses and buckboard were Joseph's.

As they approched the front entrance to the hospital, the sky was clear and the wind was calm making the day prefect for Rose to sit on her magnificent horse in front of one of the promises she had made to herself. Henry pulled his horse up beside her but did not dismount. Refusing to get off of his horse. He sat watching and waiting.

"Henry," Rose began her explanation that she should have given him along time ago. "This is my hospital, built with money given to me by Joseph Higgins. I am very rich.

As you know, I have asked Mary Rocker to run it for me and she readily said, yes." Henry removed his large old cowboy hat. He had this funny little smile on his face. Up to now he had doubted her.

⚬ Chapter 43 ⚬

The front door of the hospital suddenly opened up. Toby stepped out into the sun. He looked at Rose and each step he took was directly toward her. Rose thought she could hear her heart beating. She hoped Henry could not.

Henry was watching closely.

Toby reached up and swiftly put his hands around Rose while lifting her small body up and out of her saddle. Standing close to Henry's leg, with his arms around Rose, said, "Rose, honey, your hospital is done. Now I am ready to build your library."

Henry did not move. He sat with his jaw locked together in determination. This time he was not leaving. He was in love with Rose.

For additional copies of this or other
books written by Phyllis Collmann:
pac51crc@hickorytech.net
712-552-2375
www.collmannwarehouse.com